This book belongs to:

 _____

KNUCKLES
The Hound of Hanalei

Written by **Me**
With help from my family
Rick & Susan Dierker

Illustrations by Melinda Sandler

Done by Dogs Publishing
P.O. Box 1622
Hanalei, HI 96714
kauaidogtails@aol.com

Published by Done by Dogs Publishing.

Printed in China.

ISBN-978-0-9832386-0-7
Library of Congress Control Number: 2010943228

First hardcover printing, 2011.
Second hardcover printing, 2013.
Third hardcover printing, 2014.

IN LOVING MEMORY OF MY PAL BIG RICK

I was born on the island of Kaua'i, in Hawai'i. When I was a puppy, I remember having an *'ohana* (that's Hawaiian for family) with a *kaikua'ana* (older brother) and a *kaikuahine* (sister) around me.

One day, I was taken away from my 'ohana to a place called the Animal Shelter.

It was an okay place. There were a lot of small rooms kind of like a hotel for *ʻīlio* (dogs) and *pōpoki* (cats).

I hadn't been there long when a big *kāne* (man) came by to visit. I liked him. He smelled good, and he had big *lima* (hands) which he used to pet me.

When he left, I cried big *waimaka* (tears) because I missed him.

The next day, a pretty *wahine* (lady) came. She smelled like flowers and had a *mino'aka* (smile) when she looked at me.

But she left, too. Sitting in my small room, I was so *kaumaha* (sad) I cried all night.

And then it happened! The *kāne* with the big *lima* (I call him Big Rick) and the pretty *wahine* came back - together!

The next thing I knew, I was out of my small room and in a *ka'a* (car). I can tell you now that I was scared, but the pretty *wahine* let me rest my *po'o* (head) on her lap. I felt better and fell asleep.

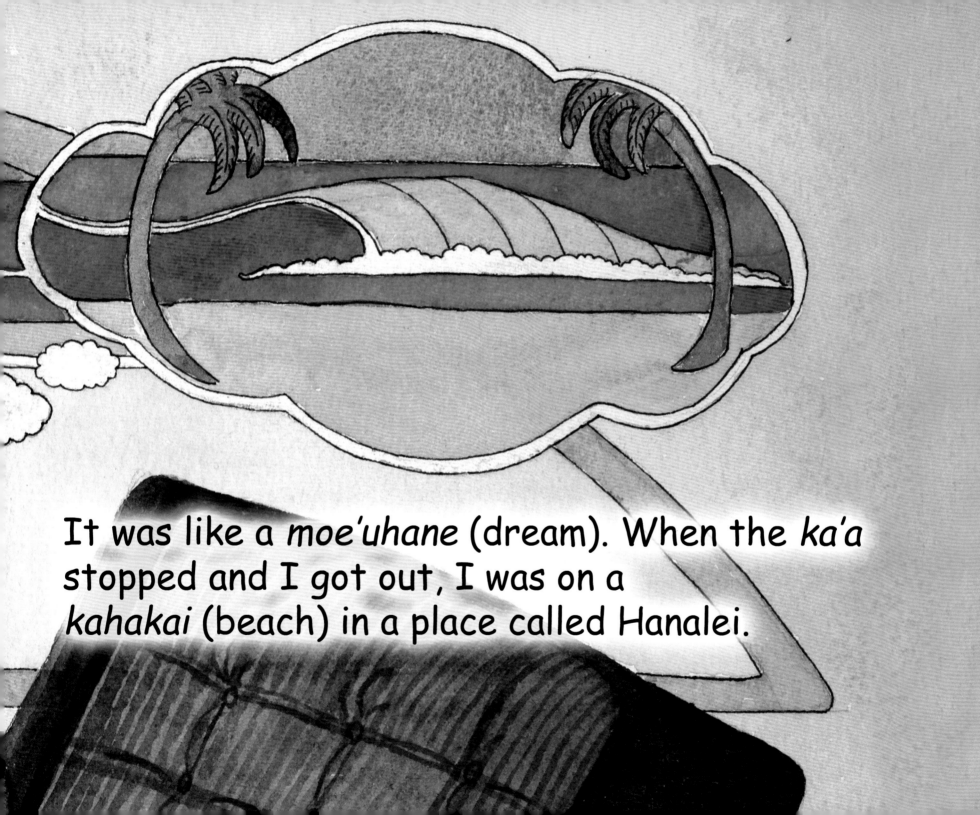

It was like a *moe'uhane* (dream). When the *ka'a* stopped and I got out, I was on a *kahakai* (beach) in a place called Hanalei.

At first, I didn't know what to do. My yard was so big I could *holo* (run) as fast as I could (I'm a fast runner) and never hit a fence!

I started to explore. The big blue *kai* (ocean) smelled like salt and roared like a lion.

And there were strange creatures for me to *pāʻani* (play) with.

I found a *kahawai* (stream). I learned it was called *Wai'oli* (happy water).

It did not sound like a lion and the water was *hu'ihu'i* (cool).

I learned to 'au (swim). I do the dog paddle.

I was starting to feel like a very lucky ʻīlio.

That night the pretty *wahine* made me the best *mea'ai* (food) ever - now I call her the Food Lady. I had my very own bowl with my new name...
"KNUCKLES".
Big Rick always wanted a hound named Knuckles. I don't know if my huge paws were the reason he chose me, but I became the *'īlio* of his dreams.

Big Rick and the Food Lady are my 'ohana and Hanalei is my kauhale (home).

MAHALO (THANK YOU)

Although some say I have a big head (and possibly an even bigger tummy)
I am forever grateful.

My heart goes out, and my tail goes all-about for:

The Kauai Humane Society
Tim, Sara & Angela Liberto
Uncle Sada
Katherine Frame Coleman
Maka'ala Warriner
Chris Cassidy
Dani Roter
Mary Kawena Pukui & Samuel H. Elbert's Hawaiian Dictionary
David & Beth London of the Poker Hill School
&
all my two- and four-legged friends
(and that three-legged guy)

Pronunciation or How to say Hawaiian words

The Hawaiian alphabet has fewer letters than English. The consonants are *h, k, l, m, n, p,* and *w.* There is also a little mark like an apostrophe (') which is called an *'okina.* It shows there is a break in the word, like saying *oh-oh* in English.

Hawaiian words have many vowels. Every syllable or word ends in a vowel. The vowels are the same as in English *a, e, i, o* and *u,* but they are pronounced differently. Sometimes the vowel sounds are stressed. A single line, which is called a kahakō over a vowel (ā) shows that the vowel sound should be longer and stronger.

The vowel sounds are:

WHEN STRESSED

ā   Like a in Far
ē   Like ay in Pay
ī   Like ee in See
ō   Like o in Sole
ū   Like oo in Moon

WHEN NOT STRESSED

a   Like a in above
e   Like e in bet
i   Like y in city
o   Like o in sole
u   Like oo in moon

Glossary of Hawaiian words

a hui hou	until we meet again	*lima*	hand
aloha	hello, goodbye, love		
'au	swim	*mahalo*	thank you
		mea'ai	food
holo	run	*mino'aka*	smile
hu'ihu'i	cool	*moe'uhane*	dream
'īlio	dog	*'ohana*	family
ka'a	car	*pau*	finished
kai	ocean	*pā'ani*	play
kahakai	beach	*po'o*	head
kahawai	stream	*pōpoki*	cat
kaikua'ana	older brother		
kaikuahine	sister	*wahine*	lady
kāne	man	*waimaka*	tears
kaumaha	sad	*Wai'oli*	happy water
kauhale	home		

ALOHA

(THAT'S THE BEST HAWAIIAN WORD EVER. IT MEANS HELLO, GOODBYE, BUT MOST OF ALL LOVE.)